My dear Rose,

Now, as I look back on the planet of the Okidians and watch it dwindle into a small twinkle of light in the distance, I can relax and smile, knowing that my new friends are safe.

Still, I marvel at how close the planet came to destruction. I don't think I will ever understand why some people are willing to risk not only their own lives but the lives of their family and friends to gain the power they crave. Such people are easy prey for the Snake.

But when swift, decisive action was needed, help came from an unexpected source, who refused to rely on others to save her planet. Although the battle with the Snake continues, I will remain full of hope as long as I continue to find generous, courageous people like her.

The Little Prince

First American edition published in 2015 by Graphic Universe™.

Le Petit Prince®

based on the masterpiece by Antoine de Saint-Exupéry

An animated series based on the novel *Le Petit Prince* by Antoine de Saint-Exupéry
Developed for television by Matthieu Delaporte, Alexandre de la Patellière, and Bertrand Gatignol
Directed by Pierre-Alain Chartier

Graphic Universe™
A division of Lerner Publishing Group, Inc.
241 First Avenue North
Minneapolis, MN 55401 USA

For reading levels and more information, look up this title at www.lernerbooks.com.

Library of Congress Cataloging-in-Publication Data

Bruneau, Clotilde.
[Planète d'Ashkabaar. English]
The planet of Ashkabaar / story by Christel Gonnard, Héloïse Cappoccia, Timothée de Fombelle ; design and illustrations by Nautilus Studio ; adaptation by Clotilde Bruneau ; translation, Anne Collins Smith and Owen Smith. — First American edition.
pages cm. — (The little prince ; #22)
ISBN 978-0-7613-8773-2 (lb : alk. paper) — ISBN 978-1-4677-6025-6 (pbk.) —
ISBN 978-1-4677-6197-0 (EB pdf)
1. Graphic novels. I. Gonnard, Christel. II. Cappoccia, Héloïse. III. Fombelle, Timothée de, 1973-
IV. Smith, Anne Collins, translator. V. Smith, Owen (Owen M.), translator. VI. Saint-Exupéry, Antoine de, 1900-1944. Petit Prince. VII. Nautilus Studio. VIII. Petit Prince (Television program) IX. Title.
PZ7.7.B8Pd 2015
741.5'944—dc23 2014038422

Manufactured in the United States of America
1 — DP — 12/31/14

THE NEW ADVENTURES
BASED ON THE MASTERPIECE BY ANTOINE DE SAINT-EXUPÉRY

The Little Prince

THE PLANET OF ASHKABAAR

Based on the animated series and an original story by Timothée de Fombelle, Christel Gonnard, and Héloïse Cappoccia

Design: Nautilus Studio
Story: Clotilde Bruneau
Artistic Direction: Didier Poli
Art: Audrey Bussi
Backgrounds: Isa Python
Coloring: Moonsun
Editing: Christine Chatal
Editorial Consultant: Didier Convard

Translation: Anne and Owen Smith

Graphic Universe™ • Minneapolis

THE LITTLE PRINCE

The Little Prince has extraordinary gifts. His sense of wonder allows him to discover what no one else can see. The Little Prince can communicate with all the beings in the universe, even the animals and plants. His powers grow over the course of his adventures.

The Prince's uniform:
When he transforms into the uniform of a prince, he is more agile and quick. When faced with difficult situations, the Little Prince also uses a sword that lets him sketch and bring to life anything from his imagination.

His sketchbook:
When he is not in his Prince's clothing, the Little Prince carries a sketchbook. When he blows on the pages, they take wing and form objects that he'll find very useful. Like his sword, it's powered by stardust collected on his travels.

FOX

A grouch, a trickster, and, so he says, interested only in his next meal, Fox is in reality the Little Prince's best friend. As such, he is always there to give him help but also just as much to help him to grow and to learn about the world.

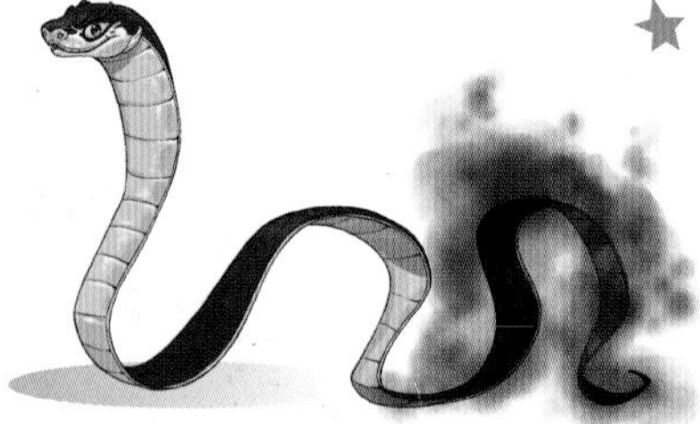

THE SNAKE

Even though the Little Prince still does not know exactly why, there can be no doubt that the Snake has set his mind to plunging the entire universe into darkness! And to accomplish his goal, this malicious being is ready to use any form of deception. However, the Snake never takes action himself. He prefers to bring out the wickedness in those beings he has chosen to bite, tempting them to put their own worlds in danger.

THE GLOOMIES

When people who have been "bitten" by the Snake have completely destroyed their own planets, they become Gloomies, slaves to their Snake master. The Gloomies act as a group and carry out the Snake's most vile orders so he can get the better of the Little Prince!

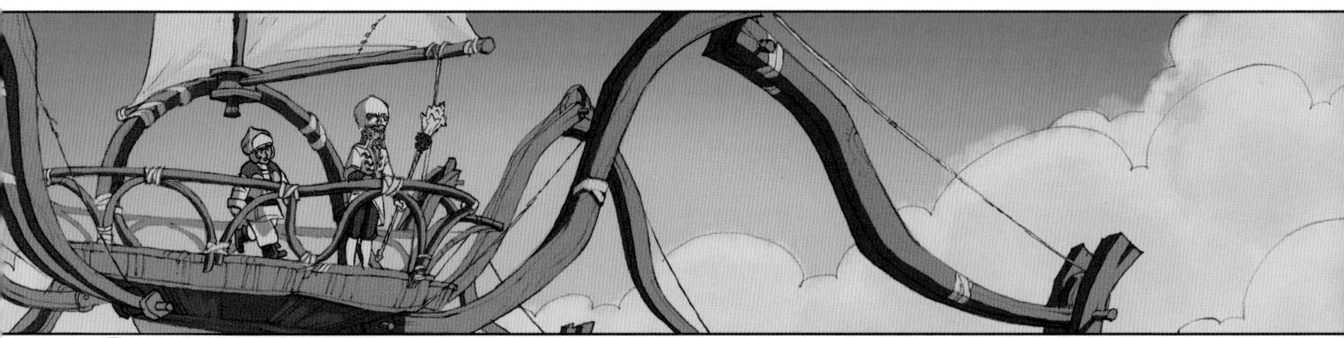

ALL SET, ASHKABAAR.
GOOD! YOU MAY BEGIN!
CHARGE!!!

ASHKABAAR!

BAD NEWS, SIR...
TELL ME-- WHAT'S WRONG?!

YOUR FAMILY IS DEAD!

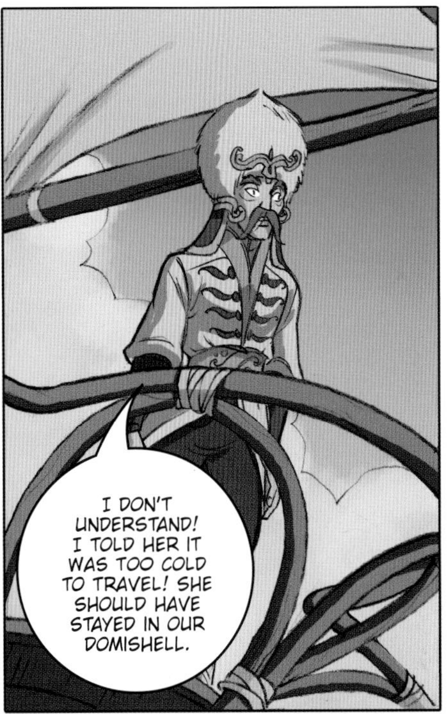

YOUR WIFE AND DAUGHTER WERE CAUGHT IN A SNOWSTORM WHEN THEY TRIED TO REACH CAMP, SIR. THEY NEVER ARRIVED.
I DON'T UNDERSTAND! I TOLD HER IT WAS TOO COLD TO TRAVEL! SHE SHOULD HAVE STAYED IN OUR DOMISHELL.

I'M TRULY SORRY.
WE'LL KEEP LOOKING FOR THEM...

WHEEEE!

I LOVE PLAYING IN THE SNOW, FOX!

ARE THOSE SEASHELLS? I'VE NEVER SEEN ANYTHING QUITE LIKE THEM!

NEITHER HAVE I! THEY'RE AS BIG AS HOUSES!
GIANT CRUSTACEANS MUST LIVE ON THIS PLANET!
WATCH OUT!

HOW RUDE--AND DANGEROUS!

THEY MAY NEED OUR HELP!

WHY SHOULD WE HELP THEM? THEY ALMOST CRUSHED US!

ARE YOU ALL RIGHT?
OH NO! I'M STUCK HERE NOW!

MY FRIEND FOX AND I WOULD BE PLEASED TO ASSIST YOU!
I'M THE LITTLE PRINCE!

CALL ME SHAAZ! I'M AFRAID THERE'S NOTHING YOU CAN DO--THE SKI PAD IS BROKEN!

NOW I WON'T BE ABLE TO DELIVER THESE ICE BLOCKS--AND THE GREAT WALL WON'T BE COMPLETED IN TIME!

WON'T A SMALL WALL WORK INSTEAD?

I'M AFRAID NOT! OUR NEIGHBORS THE CRYSTALLITES ARE ABOUT TO DECLARE WAR ON US...

...AND THE ONLY WAY TO STOP THE INVASION IS TO BUILD A TALL WALL!

WELL, THEN--THERE'S NO TIME TO LOSE!

INCREDIBLE!

AN UMBRELLA? ARE YOU SURE?
WAIT AND SEE, FOX!

IT WORKS PERFECTLY! HOW CLEVER!
THERE IT IS--THE GREAT WALL!

WE'VE BEEN BUILDING IT FOR ALMOST TWENTY YEARS, EVER SINCE ASHKABAAR SIGNED A TREATY TO END THE LAST WAR!

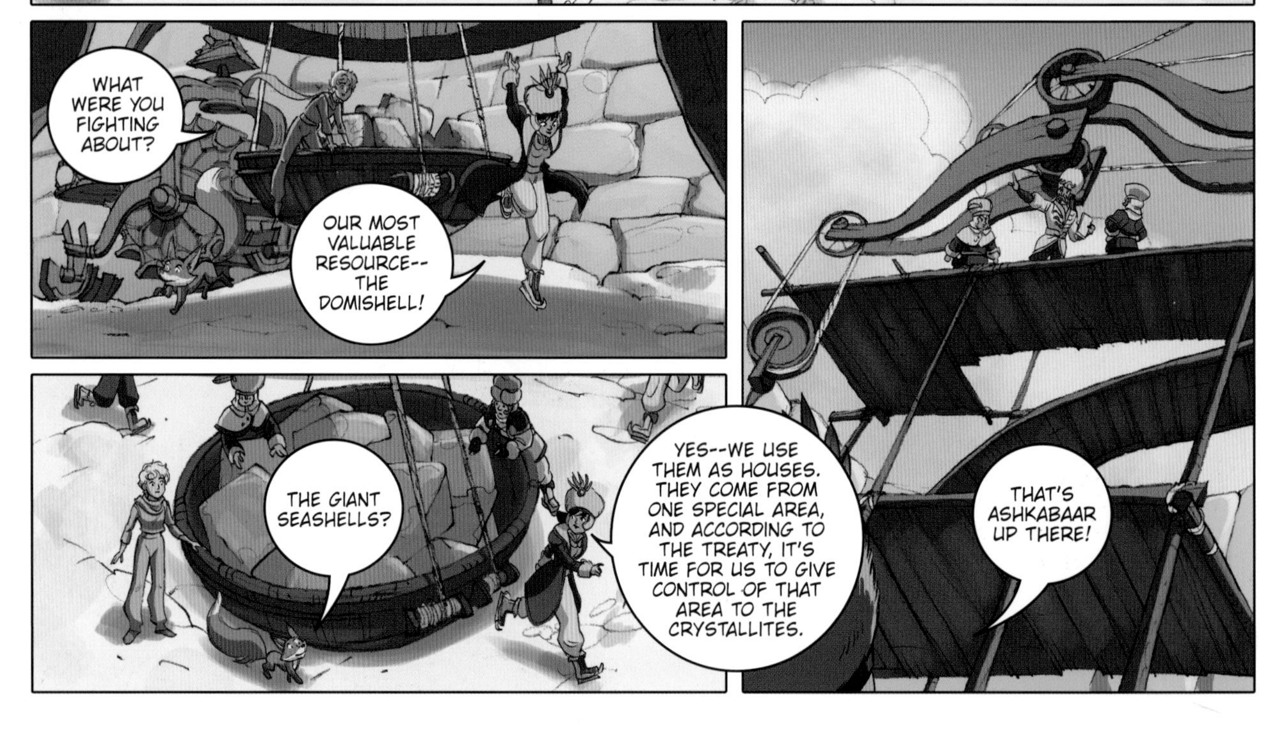
WHAT WERE YOU FIGHTING ABOUT?
OUR MOST VALUABLE RESOURCE--THE DOMISHELL!
THE GIANT SEASHELLS?
YES--WE USE THEM AS HOUSES. THEY COME FROM ONE SPECIAL AREA, AND ACCORDING TO THE TREATY, IT'S TIME FOR US TO GIVE CONTROL OF THAT AREA TO THE CRYSTALLITES.
THAT'S ASHKABAAR UP THERE!

I DON'T UNDERSTAND! WHY SHOULD THE CRYSTALLITES DECLARE WAR NOW?

IT'S THE FAULT OF RAKASH, THEIR PRINCE'S NEW COUNSELOR.

SINCE HE APPEARED, HE HAS BEEN URGING THE PRINCE TO SEIZE THE DOMISHELL'S BREEDING GROUND-- ONCE AND FOR ALL!

I WISH WE DIDN'T HAVE TO FIGHT THE CRYSTALLITES! I'M AFRAID FOR ZAAC!

IS ZAAC A BRAVE WARRIOR?

OF COURSE-- HE'S THE CRYSTALLITE PRINCE! WE'RE IN LOVE, OR AT LEAST, I THOUGHT WE WERE...

WHAT DOES ZAAC THINK ABOUT THE WAR?

I DON'T KNOW! ASHKABAAR WON'T LET ANYONE CROSS THE WALL!

I CAN'T EVEN SEND A LETTER TO ZAAC! I DON'T KNOW WHAT TO DO!

I'M SURE WE CAN HELP SOMEHOW, CAN'T WE, LITTLE PRINCE?

OF COURSE-- I KNOW JUST WHAT TO DO!

BUT WE'LL HAVE TO WAIT UNTIL IT'S DARK...

TRY NOT TO WORRY!
YOU'RE SO KIND! I JUST HOPE ZAAC STILL LOVES ME. I MISS HIM SO MUCH!

WHAT A BEAUTIFUL PENDANT! DID YOU MAKE IT YOURSELF?

NO... I'VE HAD IT FOR AS LONG AS I CAN REMEMBER.

MY ADOPTIVE MOTHER FOUND ME IN THE SNOW, WRAPPED IN FUR, AND WEARING THIS JEWEL. MY PARENTS MUST HAVE FROZEN TO DEATH DURING THE WAR. THIS IS ALL THAT REMAINS OF THEM.

BUT ENOUGH OF THE PAST-- THE FUTURE IS ALL THAT MATTERS!
JUST REMEMBER-- WE MUST WAIT UNTIL EVERYONE IS ASLEEP...

WE CAN'T WAIT MUCH LONGER! IT WILL BE DAWN SOON!

SHHH!

GOOD-- THE COAST IS CLEAR! YOU'LL BE WITH ZAAC SOON!

I CAN'T BELIEVE MY EYES!
THIS IS CERTAINLY NOT WHAT I EXPECTED!

THERE'S NO ARMY! WHERE COULD THE ENEMY HAVE GONE?

CLEARLY, THINGS ARE NOT AS THEY APPEAR! LET'S FIND OUT WHAT'S REALLY GOING ON.

LET'S FIND ZAAC!

I STILL CAN'T BELIEVE IT!

RAKASH MUST BE PLANNING A SURPRISE ATTACK! THERE'S NO OTHER EXPLANATION!

WELL, LET'S GO FIND OUT!

WE'LL NEVER GET PAST THOSE GUARDS. FOLLOW ME--ZAAC SHOWED ME A SECRET ENTRANCE.

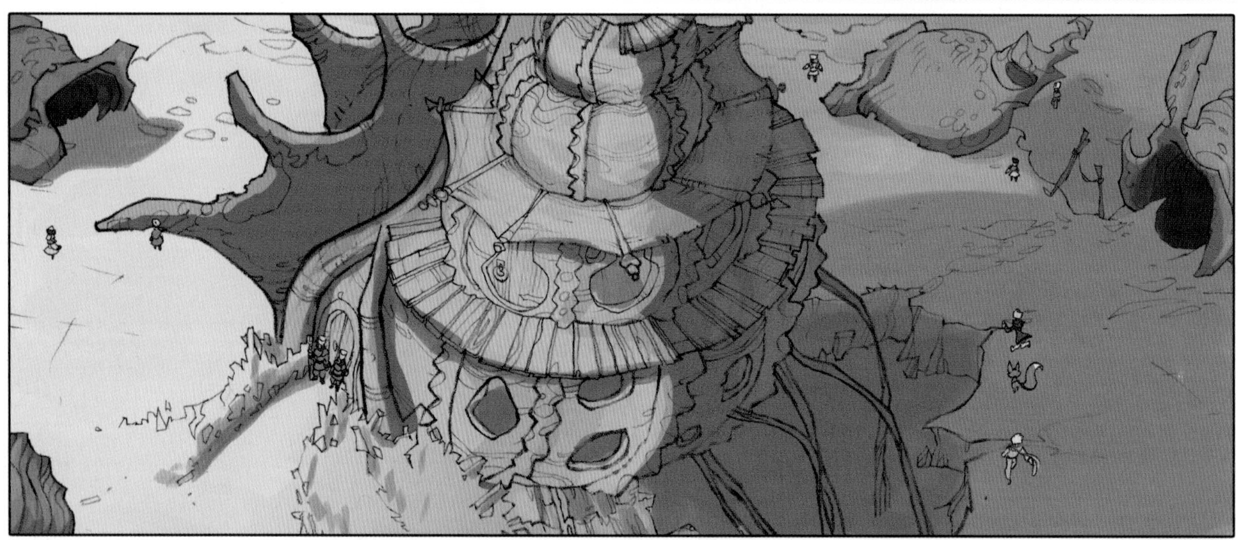

IN HERE!

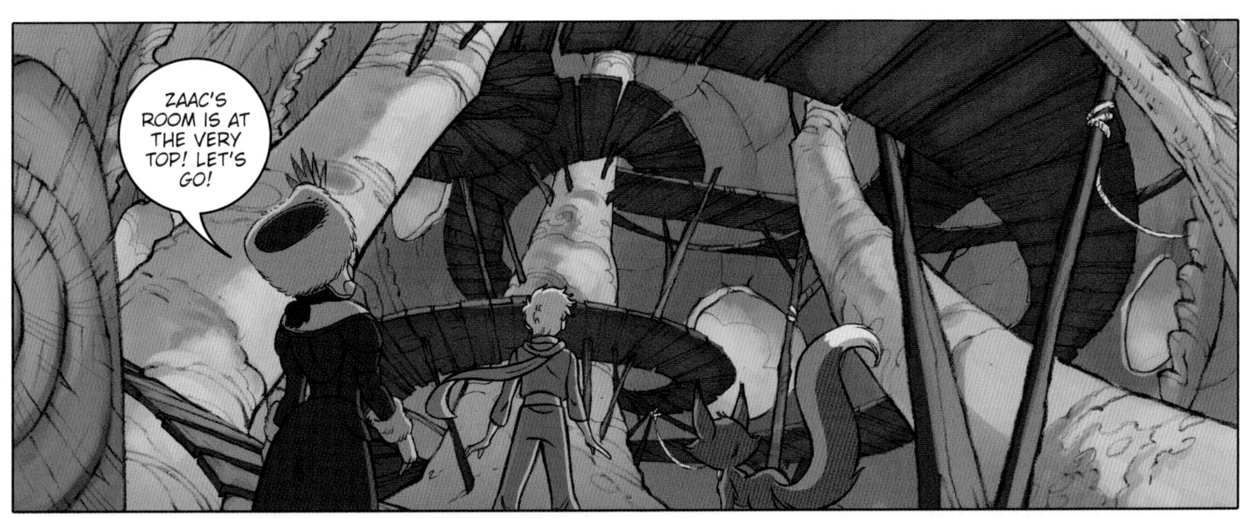
ZAAC'S ROOM IS AT THE VERY TOP! LET'S GO!

WE NEED TO BE CAREFUL!
I CAN'T WAIT TO SEE HIM!

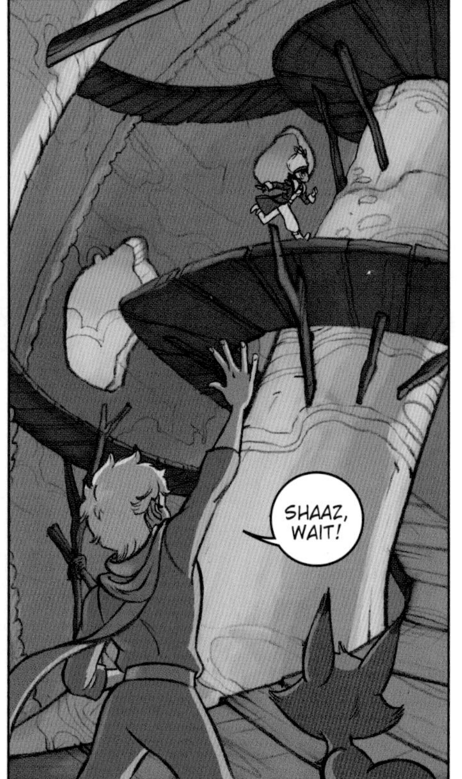
SHAAZ, WAIT!

HALT!

ARREST THIS SPY IMMEDIATELY!

RAKASH!

LET ME GO!

ZAAC!

ZAAC!
HELP ME!

SHAAZ,
IS THAT
YOU?

I MUST
HAVE
IMAGINED
IT...

NO, WAIT!
WHAT'S
THIS?

SO I
DID HEAR
HER...

SHAAZ
WAS
REALLY
HERE!

WE KNOW HOW TO DEAL WITH SPIES LIKE YOU!

SEAL THE DOOR AND THEN RETURN TO YOUR DUTIES! I NEED TIME ALONE TO THINK.

IF I'M RIGHT, RAKASH WILL LEAD US TO THE REAL VILLAIN ON THIS PLANET...
...THE SNAKE!

ARE WE FINALLY THERE?

WE MUST WAIT SILENTLY UNTIL HE'S GONE!

I WONDER WHAT WE'LL FIND UP HERE!

THIS IS NOT WHAT I EXPECTED!

ASHKABAAR?!

FOX! WE'VE CROSSED BACK UNDER THE WALL!

LOOK--THE WOMAN IN THE PHOTO HAS THE SAME PENDANT AS SHAAZ!

OF COURSE! IT ALL MAKES SENSE!

TELL ME!

NOT YET-- IT'S JUST A HUNCH!

YOU'VE GOT TO SEE THIS!

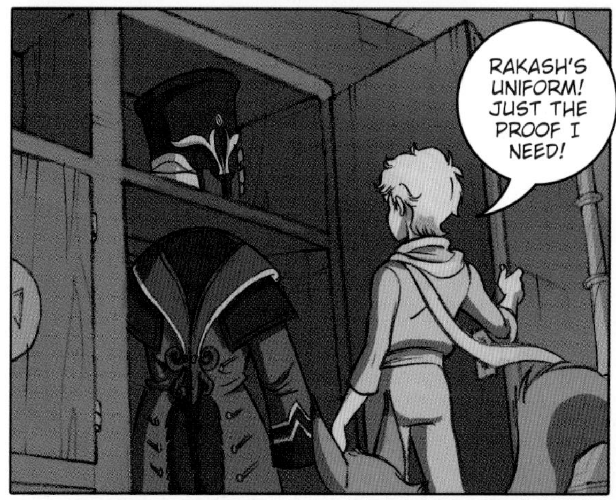
RAKASH'S UNIFORM! JUST THE PROOF I NEED!

RAKASH AND ASHKABAAR ARE THE SAME PERSON! IT'S THE ONLY EXPLANATION.
WE'VE LOOKED EVERYWHERE-- NO ONE HAS SEEN HER.

SHE MUST HAVE CROSSED THE WALL AND JOINED THE ENEMY!

YOU'RE JUMPING TO CONCLUSIONS! SHAAZ IS NO TRAITOR. SHE'S SIMPLY GONE TO SEE THE MAN SHE LOVES.

IN FACT, SHE'S BEEN ARRESTED AS A SPY!
OH NO!

I'M NOT SURE I CAN NEGOTIATE HER RELEASE-- RAKASH IS TOO UNREASONABLE!
PLEASE TRY!

I KNEW IT! IF HE WASN'T RAKASH, HOW COULD HE KNOW ABOUT SHAAZ'S ARREST?

THIS INFORMATION IS CONFIDENTIAL. SPEAK OF IT TO NO ONE! WE CAN'T AFFORD TO ALARM THE PEOPLE AT THIS CRITICAL TIME.

RETURN TO YOUR DUTIES-- I NEED TIME ALONE TO THINK.

WE MUST HURRY BACK AND RELEASE SHAAZ BEFORE ASHKABAAR TURNS BACK INTO RAKASH!

WHAT DO WE DO ABOUT ASHKABAAR?

FOR THE MOMENT-- NOTHING! I THINK I FINALLY UNDERSTAND WHAT'S GOING ON HERE.

WHY SO SSSOLEMN, MY FRIEND?

I KNOW! SHE IS A MENACE TO OUR PLANS... HSSS...
THERE'S A PROBLEM WITH SHAAZ.

WHAT WILL ZAAC DO IF HE FINDS OUT THAT YOUR PEOPLE--THE SPHEROLITES--AREN'T PREPARED FOR A WAR?

MORE IMPORTANTLY, WHAT WILL YOUR PEOPLE DO IF THEY FIND OUT THAT THIS WAR IS A COMPLETE LIE? THEY WON'T HAVE A CHOICE!

I KNOW! THEY WILL ABANDON ME, AND I WILL BE ALL ALONE-- AGAIN!

IT'S A SHAME THAT SHAAZ DISOBEYED YOUR ORDER... YOU HAD TO LOCK HER UP!

IF SHE REVEALS WHAT SHE HAS SEEN, BOTH WILL LEARN THE TRUTH--AND EVERYONE WILL SHUN YOU.

DO YOU WANT TO END UP ALONE, ASHKABAAR?

OF COURSE NOT!

THEN YOU KNOW WHAT YOU HAVE TO DO!

I STILL DON'T UNDERSTAND WHY ASHKABAAR WANTS BOTH SIDES TO BE AFRAID OF EACH OTHER!

PERHAPS HE NEEDS TO FEEL NEEDED...

SHAAZ!

HOW CAN WE SET HER FREE?
I'M AFRAID SHAAZ WILL HAVE TO WAIT...

WATCH OUT, SHAAZ! TAKE COVER!

WELL, WHAT ARE YOU WAITING FOR?

SHAAZ?!

WOW! WHAT AN EXPLOSION!

I'M GLAD YOU'RE ALL RIGHT!

I DON'T THINK THEY'LL BOTHER US AGAIN!

LISTEN CAREFULLY, SHAAZ--FOX AND I HAVE SOME IMPORTANT NEWS TO TELL YOU!
WHAT? HAS SOMETHING HAPPENED TO ZAAC?

NO--BUT RAKASH IS ASHKABAAR IN DISGUISE!

WHAT?! THAT'S IMPOSSIBLE!

WE HAVE ALL THE EVIDENCE WE NEED! WE EVEN FOLLOWED RAKASH ALL THE WAY BACK TO ASHKABAAR'S ROOM!

I CAN HARDLY BELIEVE IT!
WAIT-- THERE'S MORE...

WHEN WE WERE IN ASHKABAAR'S ROOM, WE FOUND THIS FAMILY PHOTO.
POOR ASHKABAAR! HE LOST HIS WHOLE FAMILY A LONG TIME AGO...

LOOK AT THE PENDANT HIS WIFE IS WEARING. HAVE YOU SEEN IT BEFORE?

WHY... YES! IT'S MY PENDANT!
DO YOU REALIZE WHAT THIS MEANS?

ASHKABAAR IS YOUR FATHER!

HE IS?
THE PENDANT PROVES IT! BUT WHERE DID IT GO?

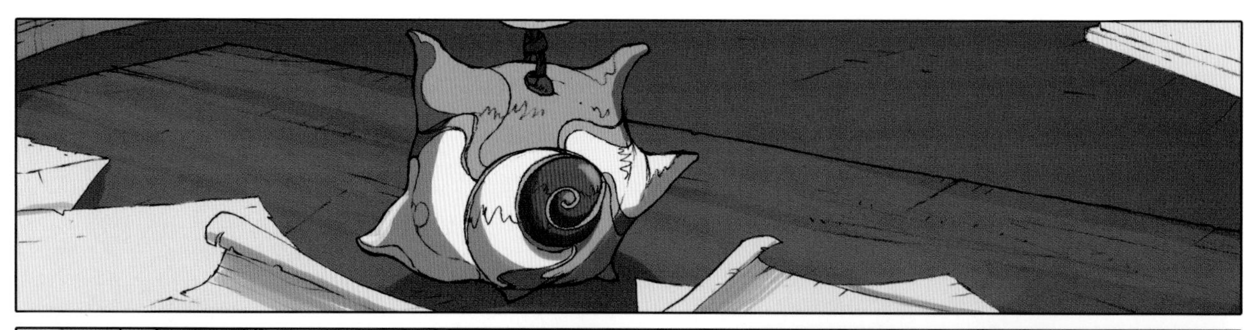

WHERE ARE YOU, SHAAZ?

ZAAC!

I'M GLAD YOU FOUND MY PENDANT! I LOST IT DURING MY ARREST!
ARREST?! WHAT ARE YOU TALKING ABOUT?

I CAME TO SEE YOU, BUT INSTEAD, I WAS ARRESTED BY RAKASH-- I MEAN, ASHKABAAR!

YOU'RE NOT MAKING ANY SENSE!
SHAAZ IS TRYING TO TELL YOU THAT WE'VE MADE A CRUCIAL DISCOVERY: ASHKABAAR AND RAKASH ARE THE SAME PERSON!

FOR SOME REASON WE DON'T QUITE UNDERSTAND, ASHKABAAR IS TRYING TO CONVINCE BOTH SIDES THAT A WAR IS ABOUT TO BEGIN!

INCREDIBLE...

NOW I KNOW WHY RAKASH CONFINED ME TO MY ROOM!
HOW DID HE MANAGE TO DO THAT?

HE SAID IT WAS FOR MY OWN SAFETY. HE TOLD ME THAT THE SPHEROLITES WERE PLOTTING TO ATTACK US.

WE HAVE LONG FEARED THAT THE SPHEROLITES WOULD NOT HONOR THE TREATY AND GIVE US CONTROL OVER THE DOMISHELL BREEDING GROUND.

OUR DOMISHELLS ARE SO OLD THAT THEY'RE FALLING APART... I HAD TO TRUST HIM!

WHY DIDN'T YOU TELL ME?

WE WERE IN NO POSITION TO DEFEAT THE SPHEROLITES. I COULD NOT RISK ANYTHING THAT MIGHT PROVOKE AN ATTACK BY ASHKABAAR!

NOW THAT THE CAT'S OUT OF THE BAG, WHAT DO WE DO?

WE MUST STOP ASHKABAAR'S PLOT, WHATEVER IT TAKES.

BUT HOW? NEITHER SIDE WILL TRUST THE OTHER!

THE FIRST STEP IS TO IDENTIFY THE PROBLEM.

THE WALL PREVENTS EACH SIDE FROM LEARNING ABOUT THE OTHER! SO-- DESTROY THE WALL!

I AGREE! BUT TIME IS SHORT AND THE WALL IS TALL!
DON'T WORRY! I HAVE A FRIEND WHO CAN HELP.

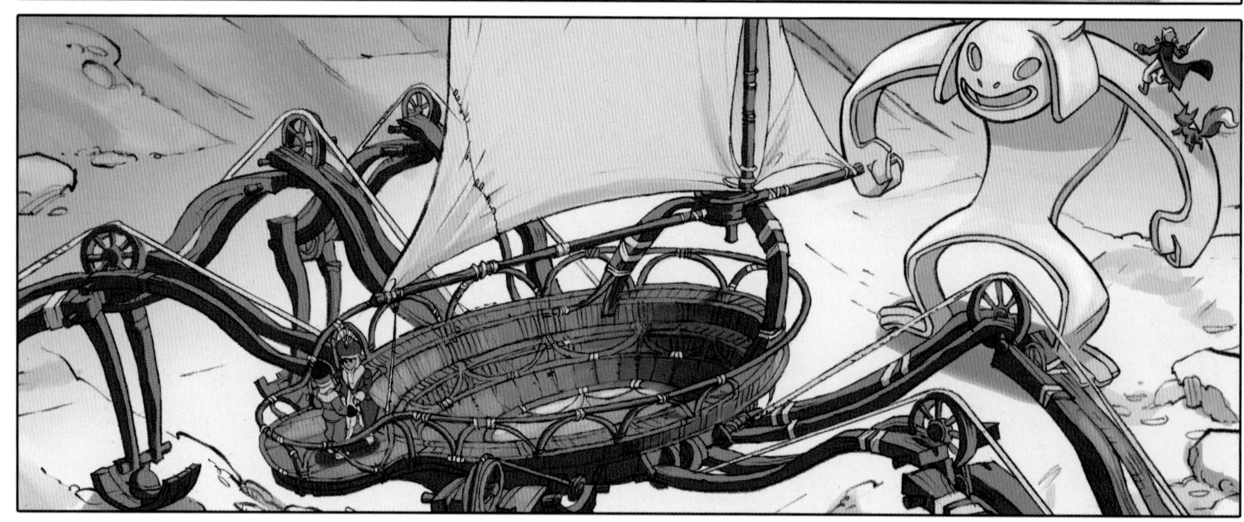

LET'S GO!

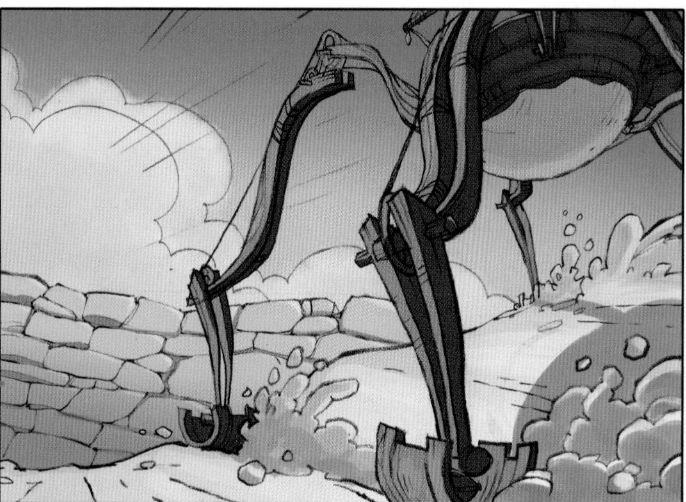

WE'RE BEING ATTACKED!

THE ENEMY HAS DESTROYED THE WALL!
RUN FOR YOUR LIVES!

WAIT! I DON'T SEE ANY ENEMY SOLDIERS!

WHAT?!

WE'D BETTER EXPLAIN, SHAAZ!

I DON'T UNDERSTAND! WHERE'S YOUR ARMY?
WE NEVER HAD AN ARMY!
IT'S ALL REALLY CONFUSING! FIRST OF ALL--
WAIT, SHAAZ!

I AM ZAAC, PRINCE OF THE CRYSTALLITES! I'M HERE TO BRING PEACE TO OUR TWO PEOPLES!

HAVE YOU FINALLY DECIDED TO NEGOTIATE?
CAN WE FINALLY SLEEP IN PEACE?

WHAT'S GOING ON HERE?

I AM ZAAC, PRINCE OF THE CRYSTALLITES! MY COUNSELOR, RAKASH, HAS BEEN PUT IN PRISON FOR HIGH TREASON! WE WILL NEVER SPEAK OF HIM AGAIN!
BUT HOW--

THERE'S NOTHING TO PREVENT A LASTING PEACE NOW, IS THERE?

NO, I SUPPOSE NOT--NOW THAT THE WALL IS GONE.

PERFECT! THE DETAILS OF A NEW TREATY CAN WAIT UNTIL LATER. WE HAVE MORE IMPORTANT NEWS TO SHARE WITH YOU.

I'VE WORN THIS PENDANT SINCE I WAS FOUND AS A BABY, ALONE IN THE SNOW!

DO YOU RECOGNIZE IT?

I GAVE IT TO MY WIFE MANY YEARS AGO WHEN OUR DAUGHTER WAS BORN.

BUT HOW?!
WE HAVE MANY THINGS TO DISCUSS, BUT LET US SPEAK IN PRIVATE.

I CAN'T BELIEVE YOU'RE REALLY ALIVE!

I'M NOT ALONE!

THERE ARE MANY THINGS I STILL DON'T UNDERSTAND...
WHY MAKE EVERYONE FEAR A NEW WAR?

BEFORE I LEARNED ABOUT SHAAZ, I HAD NO FAMILY--ONLY MY PEOPLE...

ONCE I FULFILLED THE TERMS OF THE TREATY, MY PEOPLE WOULD HAVE NO NEED FOR ME. I WOULD BE USELESS, FORGOTTEN... ALONE. THEN I MET A STRANGE CREATURE--

THE SNAKE! GRRRR...

THE SNAKE USED YOUR DEEPEST FEARS TO POISON YOUR MIND. YOU MUST LEARN TO TRUST OTHERS-- THEY CAN EASE YOUR FEARS.

MY ONLY FEAR NOW IS THAT YOU WON'T FORGIVE ME!

THEN FEAR NO MORE! FAMILY MEMBERS MUST LEARN TO FORGIVE EACH OTHER.

ZAAC!

NOTHING WOULD GIVE ME MORE JOY THAN TO WELCOME YOU INTO MY FAMILY. TODAY, I GAIN BOTH A DAUGHTER AND A SON!

I AM HONORED TO ANNOUNCE THE MARRIAGE OF PRINCE ZAAC AND MY DAUGHTER, SHAAZ. LET OUR TWO PEOPLES, NOW JOINED, NEVER AGAIN BE SEPARATED!

DO YOU THINK WE'LL EVER SEE THE LITTLE PRINCE AND FOX AGAIN?

I DON'T KNOW, BUT I'M SURE WE'LL NEVER FORGET THEM!

IT'S A SHAME WE MISSED THE WEDDING! THE BUFFET WOULD HAVE BEEN MAGNIFICENT!
EACH TIME I LOOK AT THIS PENDANT, I WILL REMEMBER SHAAZ AND ZAAC AND WISH THEM WELL!

Read all the Books in *The Little Prince* series

Book 1: The Planet of Wind
Book 2: The Planet of the Firebird
Book 3: The Planet of Music
Book 4: The Planet of Jade
Book 5: The Star Snatcher's Planet
Book 6: The Planet of the Night Globes
Book 7: The Planet of the Overhearers
Book 8: The Planet of the Tortoise Driver
Book 9: The Planet of the Giant
Book 10: The Planet of Trainiacs
Book 11: The Planet of Libris
Book 12: The Planet of Ludokaa
Book 13: The Planet of Tear-Eaters
Book 14: The Planet of the Grand Buffoon
Book 15: The Planet of the Gargand
Book 16: The Planet of Gehom
Book 17: The Planet of the Bubble Gob
Book 18: The Planet of Time
Book 19: The Planet of the Cublix
Book 20: The Planet of Coppelius
Book 21: The Planet of Okidians
Book 22: The Planet of Ashkabaar